In Memory Of

Ruth M. Seibert

Presented by

Jean E. Gilmore

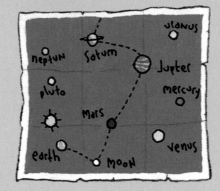

For my good friend Darran—R.C.

First published in Great Britain by Bloomsbury Publishing Plc, under the title *Maybe One Day*.

Printed in Hong Kong

First U.S. Edition

1 3 5 7 9 10 8 6 4 2

Library of Congress Cataloging-in-Publication data on file.
ISBN 0-7868-0732-6

This book is set in
Goudy Infant.

One Day, Daddy

Frances Thomas

Illustrated by
Ross Collins

Hyperion Books for Children
New York

"I've got this problem,"

said Little Monster.

"I'm sorry to hear that,"

said Father Monster.

"What's the problem?"

"Well," said Little Monster, "maybe one day I'll want to be an explorer."

"Maybe you will," said Father Monster. "Is that a problem?"

"Yes, it is," said Little Monster.

"You see, Daddy, if I'm an explorer, I'll have to leave you and Mommy behind."

"Well," said Father Monster,

"maybe we could come with you."

"Don't be silly," said Little Monster. "Explorers don't take their mommies and daddies along with them."

"No, I guess not," said Father Monster. "So where will you **explore?**"

"Well,
I'd really really like
to go to the moon.
Did you know that on the
moon you can jump as high
as a house because there's less
gravity to weigh you down?"

"You might
bounce
all
the
way

back
into
space,"

said
Father Monster.

"I said
as high as a
house,"
said Little Monster.
"I didn't say
as high as
space."

"Don't forget to look up at the sky.
You might see Mommy and me
waving from Earth,"
said Father Monster.

"You'd be much too far away to see," said Little Monster.
"But I would send you a piece of moonrock as a present."

"Thank you very much,"
said Father Monster.

"We'd put it on the mantel next to the clock."

Mummy & Daddy Monster
House on hill the Earth.

"And when I've finished on the moon," said Little Monster,

"I'll go to Mars."

"Watch out for all those Martians,"
said Father Monster.

"There aren't any Martians,"
said Little Monster.

"Are you sure about that?"

said Father Monster.

"Of course I am,"

said Little Monster.

"Well, I'm almost sure."

"Then maybe I'll go to Jupiter.

"Did you know Jupiter has sixteen moons?"

"That's
kind of greedy
of Jupiter,"
said
Father Monster,

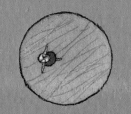

"when we
have only
one."

"And it has
a big red spot,"
said Little Monster,
"and nobody knows
what's in it."

"Maybe
a big RED dragon,"
said Father Monster,
"waiting
to eat you up."

"Well, I would probably avoid him," said Little Monster.

"And then I'll go to Saturn and see the rings."

"Be careful you don't slide off,"

said Father Monster.

"Then maybe
I'll look for a
meteor shower."
"Make sure you
take your umbrella,"
said Father Monster.

"And if I see a comet with a long, long, shining tail, I'll jump on it and ride

all the way
out into space,

beyond
the planets,

until
I get to the
stars."

"That's a long, long way to go," said Father Monster.

"But I would have to go a long, long way to get to the stars, wouldn't I?

"And then,
I'll look for a star that
nobody has ever found before,"

said Little Monster.

"And if I like it,
maybe I'll stay there for a while."

"Won't you be lonely there?"
said Father Monster.

"Yes, but you have to be lonely
to do some things," said Little Monster.

"And will you come back to us one day?"

"Oh yes, one day I'll come back, Daddy."